ROLLIN'

RIGHT ALONG!

Olvina Flies

Written and illustrated by

Grace Lin

Henry Holt and Company

New York

Henry Holt and Company, LLC
Publishers since 1866
115 West 18th Street, New York, New York 10011
www.henryholt.com

Library of Congress Cataloging-in-Publication Data
Lin, Grace. Olvina flies / written and illustrated by Grace Lin.
Summary: When Olvina, a chicken, receives an invitation to the annual Bird Convention
in Hawaii, Will the pig and a fellow passenger help her to overcome her fear of flying.
[1. Fear—Fiction. 2. Voyages and travels—Fiction. 3. Chickens—Fiction. 4. Pigs—Fiction.]
I. Title. PZ7.L644 Ol 2003 [Fic]—dc21 2002008090
ISBN 0-8050-6711-6 / First Edition—2003 / Designed by Donna Mark
Printed in the United States of America on acid-free paper. ∞

1 3 5 7 9 10 8 6 4 2

The artist used gouache on Arches hot-pressed paper
to create the illustrations for this book.

For Boston, the friends I have there, and
the airplanes I travel in to visit them

Every Thursday, Will came over to Olvina's house for tea. Today Olvina had a letter on the table.

"Look, Olvina," Will said. "You've got an invitation to the Tenth Annual Bird Convention. And it's in Hawaii!"

"I know," Olvina said glumly. "I can't go."

"You can't?" asked Will. "Why not?"

"Because I am a chicken," Olvina sighed.

"So?" asked Will.

"Because," burst Olvina, "to get to Hawaii you have to FLY over the ocean and CHICKENS CAN'T FLY! The Bird Convention made a mistake inviting me."

"But Olvina," Will protested, "it's the Bird Convention, not the Flying Bird Convention. You can still go. Just take an airplane."

"An airplane?" said Olvina. "No, I couldn't do that. I've never been on an airplane."

"Oh, Olvina," Will moaned. "Don't be such a chicken."

"But I am a chicken," Olvina said to herself after Will left. As she sat down at the kitchen table, Olvina began to think about all the things she had missed because she couldn't fly. She started making a list. There was that Egg Reunion in March and Aunt Mabel's Feathered Friend Party. . . .

By the time Olvina had finished the list, the whole kitchen was filled with paper. Olvina looked at the mess and reached for the phone.

"Will," she huffed, "you were right. I should go to the Bird Convention. I'm taking that airplane!"

The next day Olvina went to buy her ticket. Since the airline didn't get many bird passengers, they gave her a special discount. Olvina blushed as she bought her ticket. "It's so embarrassing that I can't fly," she thought.

Mom & Will

Olvina was still packing the night before her flight when Will called.

"Will," Olvina said, "I don't know if I can do this after all. I can't decide how many pairs of socks I should bring, I've lost my sunglasses, and my suitcase won't close. Maybe I shouldn't go. Chickens aren't supposed to fly."

"Relax," said Will. "You can do it. Pigs aren't supposed to fly either, but I do every year to visit my mother. I'll be there tomorrow to drive you to the airport."

The following morning Olvina and Will drove to the airport. Olvina stared in wonder.

"It's very busy at an airport," she mumbled to herself.

First Olvina had to check in.

"All you need to do is show your ticket and identification and give them your luggage," Will assured her. "Don't worry, it's easy."

Unfortunately, checking in did not go smoothly. Olvina accidentally packed her ticket in her suitcase and had to unpack everything to find it. The line behind Olvina grew and grew. The attendant giggled when she saw Olvina's polka-dotted panties.

Then Olvina had to pass through the security detectors. Will stayed behind because he wasn't flying.

"Just watch the signs—they'll tell you where to go," he called. "And have a good time, Olvina!"

Plane to Hawaii →
this way

Olvina saw the signs to her airplane. Passengers were already lined up.

She followed the passengers through a doorway and down a long hallway. At the end of the hall she could see the opening of the airplane. A flight attendant took her ticket and brought Olvina to her seat.

Olvina sat down and looked out the window. They were very high up.

"Please fasten your seat belt," said the attendant. "We will be taking off soon."

"*Taking off!*" Olvina winced. She clamped her seat belt tightly around her. The attendant then played a video about air safety. Olvina was starting to feel very nervous. "Maybe I should get off the plane," she thought.

Too late—they were moving! Olvina closed her eyes. The plane jolted and grumbled and whistled. "Oh no!" Olvina groaned as she clutched the armrests.

Then the noise stopped. Olvina's ears felt strange and kind of stuffy. She opened her eyes.

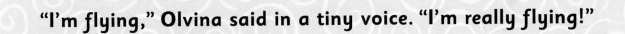

"I'm flying," Olvina said in a tiny voice. "I'm really flying!"

"Would you like some gum?" the passenger next to her asked. "It helps get rid of that popping noise in your ears."

"Thank you," said Olvina.

"I'm glad I have to take an airplane to the Bird Convention," her neighbor said. "All the other birds look so tired when they fly by."

"You're going to the Bird Convention?" Olvina gasped. "Me too!"

"Really?" said the penguin, smiling. "My name is Hailey."

Olvina and Hailey talked and talked. They talked through the airplane dinner and movie. Olvina told Hailey that this was her first flight, and Hailey told Olvina about how it was too far to swim to Hawaii. Later Hailey comforted Olvina as the plane landed. "Don't worry," Hailey said. "All that bumping is normal."

Olvina and Hailey claimed their luggage together and even shared a taxi to the hotel.

"We're going to have such fun at the convention," Hailey told Olvina. "I'm so glad you decided to come!"

"You know," Olvina said, "I am too."

Hailey and I relaxing

Hailey and I snorkeling

drinking coconuts

At the beach

Dear Will,
    I'm having a great time - wait until you see my pictures! ☺
        See you soon!
            ♡ Olvina

P.S. Flying was easy!

To:
    WILL GELATO
    4 FROSTING CIRCLE
    PACYWORKS VILLAGE